JUDITH VIGNA

My Big Sister
Takes Drugs

ALBERT WHITMAN & COMPANY, NILES, ILLINOIS

For Chris, and with special thanks to
counselors Adele, Pat, and Mary.

Library of Congress Cataloging-in-Publication Data
Vigna, Judith.
My big sister takes drugs/
story and pictures by Judith Vigna.
p.   cm.
Summary: When the police bring home Paul's
sister Tina, who was found taking drugs in the
park, a nightmare begins for the family, and
Paul's new friendship with José and his plans
for soccer camp both seem lost.
ISBN 0-8075-5317-4
[1. Drug abuse—Fiction.   2. Brothers and
sisters—Fiction.] I. Title.
PZ7.V67My   1990   89-70736
[Fic]—dc20   CIP
                                                      AC

Text and illustrations © 1990 by Judith Vigna.
Published in 1990 by Albert Whitman & Company,
5747 West Howard Street, Niles, Illinois 60648.
Published simultaneously in Canada by General
Publishing, Limited, Toronto.
All rights reserved.
Printed in the United States of America.
10 9 8 7 6 5 4 3 2 1

The illustrations are watercolor.
The text typeface is Horley Old Style.

My sister, Tina, made some new friends last fall.
She met them when we moved because of my
mom's new job. Tina and her friends hung out
in the park where I practice soccer.

Once I kicked my ball into the trees and saw
them drinking beer and stuff. They told me to
get lost.

I hated that.

Before, I was Tina's best friend. Lots of times she'd walk me home from school and play with me till Mom and Dad got back. But after she changed, she'd sometimes skip school and forget me. I had to get my own key, just in case.

New Year's Eve, Tina tried to give me a little red pill. She said it would make me feel better. Only I didn't take it. I wasn't sick or anything.

"Remember what Mom and Dad said," I told her. "Never take pills unless the doctor says it's okay."

"You're chicken," Tina said. "All the kids do it."

When I told Mom about the pill, she grounded Tina for a week. Tina called me a snitch and said she'd never play with me again.

I'm not lonely when I'm playing soccer. Dad's promised to send me to soccer camp so I'll be ready for A Team next year. He says I'm a great goalie. That's because I have big hands.

There's a boy on the team I like a lot. His family lives on our block.

"Can José come and see my pennant collection?" I asked Mom.

"Of course," she said. "We can make supper a cookout."

"Be home by six," Mom told Tina. "Paul's new friend is coming over. We're having a cookout."

"I'm busy tonight," Tina snapped.

Mom got mad. "You think you're so cool, you and your friends! But you're selfish and rude!"

And then Mom yelled at *Dad*. "Why don't *you* talk to her," she said, "instead of burying your head in the newspaper!"

I got mad, too. "It's my cookout. What about *me*?" Then Mom hugged me and Dad and Tina, all of us warm and snug like it used to be.

"I hate what is happening to our family!" Mom cried.

Tina squished my hair. "Okay, Squirt. I'll come to your dumb cookout."

Later, while Dad barbecued on the porch, I showed José my pennant collection. "I'm going to sleep-away soccer camp this summer," I told him.

"That's cool," José said. "I wish I could go."

Mom kept looking at her watch. "It's after seven. Tina promised to be home by six." I don't know why she got so nervous. Tina's never home on time.

Finally, I couldn't wait. "José's hungry," I said. We ate like two lions. Franks and three-bean salad and raspberry soda. Mom didn't eat at all.

Suddenly, I heard a car door bang, then loud voices and yelling.

"Stay where you are, boys!" Dad ordered. He and Mom ran out front.

I had to peek. What if the house was on fire?

It was Tina! A police lady was trying to hold her. My sister was kicking and cursing and all dirty. Everyone could hear. It was terrible.

"We picked up your daughter in the park," the cop told Dad. "Her friends ran off. Seems they were smoking crack. We found this empty vial." (That's a little plastic tube that the drug crack comes in. Our teacher showed us once.)

"The other kids were doing crack, not me!" Tina screamed.

It's good they let her go. I was scared they'd take her to jail.

After the cops left, Mom acted almost as weird as Tina. "So that's where the money from my purse went!" she shrieked. "To buy drugs!" She took my sister to her room and stayed until Tina stopped shouting and crashing around.

Dad just sat at the picnic table and stared. "Not my Tina!" he said over and over.

José's eyes were round like soccer balls. "I have to go," he stammered. "My mom's waiting."

"Tina *said* it wasn't her!" I yelled. But he ran out the gate.

Now I'd never make any new friends, ever.

A few days later, Dad took my sister away. I was glad. Tina was getting so mean I was scared she'd hurt me.

"She's gone to a special hospital where they'll treat her drug problem," Mom explained. "She'll be there a long time."

Then she said, "It's going to cost a lot of money. I'm afraid we'll have to postpone soccer camp."

I was so mad I cried. "I *hate* Tina! José doesn't want to be my friend, and now I can't go to camp. *I* wasn't bad!"

Mom held me. "No, Sweetheart. And Tina's not bad, either. The drugs are making her do those terrible things. She loves you, but she's very sick. She chose to take crack from her friends, and now she can't stop. Without help she may die."

That was *really* scary. Maybe snitching on her wasn't so bad, after all.

Practice day came. I decided to go, even though I felt funny about seeing José.

"You're sad, Paul. Something wrong?" Coach asked.

I wasn't supposed to say anything, but I just had to. "I'll never make A Team," I told him. "We had to put off soccer camp because my sister's in a drug hospital and Mom says we can't have both."

I thought he'd hate me, too, but he didn't. "That's tough, Paul. Drugs hurt everyone," he said.

Then he made me feel even better. "We'll practice extra, just you and me. Should I ask José to help?"

I don't think José was thrilled, but he likes Coach. He fielded the balls Coach kicked at me, and I made some neat saves.

"If you two keep working together like this you'll *both* make A Team," Coach said, beaming. José looked pleased, but he didn't say anything.

After supper, José stopped by my house. "I heard you and Coach talking. I'm sorry about soccer camp." Then he gave me a pennant he'd made. It said CAMP JOSÉ-PAUL. "Let's go for A Team!" he said, and grinned.

I asked Dad if we could use his old tent for camp headquarters. "Sure," he said. "We'll pitch it in the yard, and if José's parents agree, he can sleep over tonight."

I was scared they'd say no. "Tell your mom Tina's away and she's getting better," I said to José.

I really hope my sister gets well. She was gone a long time. Now she's home, but she has to go to meetings practically forever so she won't get back on drugs. Mom and Dad take her there. And I'm left with a sitter.

"Sorry you'll be on your own again, Squirt," Tina says, hugging me.

I don't mind *too* much. Tina's lonelier than me. She had to give up her druggie friends, and she misses them. I don't know why. They all acted like they cared more about drugs than each other, though Mom says they need help, too.

I hope Tina remembers. Then maybe she'll get a *real* friend—

like mine.